DATE DUE

PRO SPORTS CHAMPIONSHIPS

NCAA BASKETBALL CHAMPIONSHIP

Annalise Bekkering

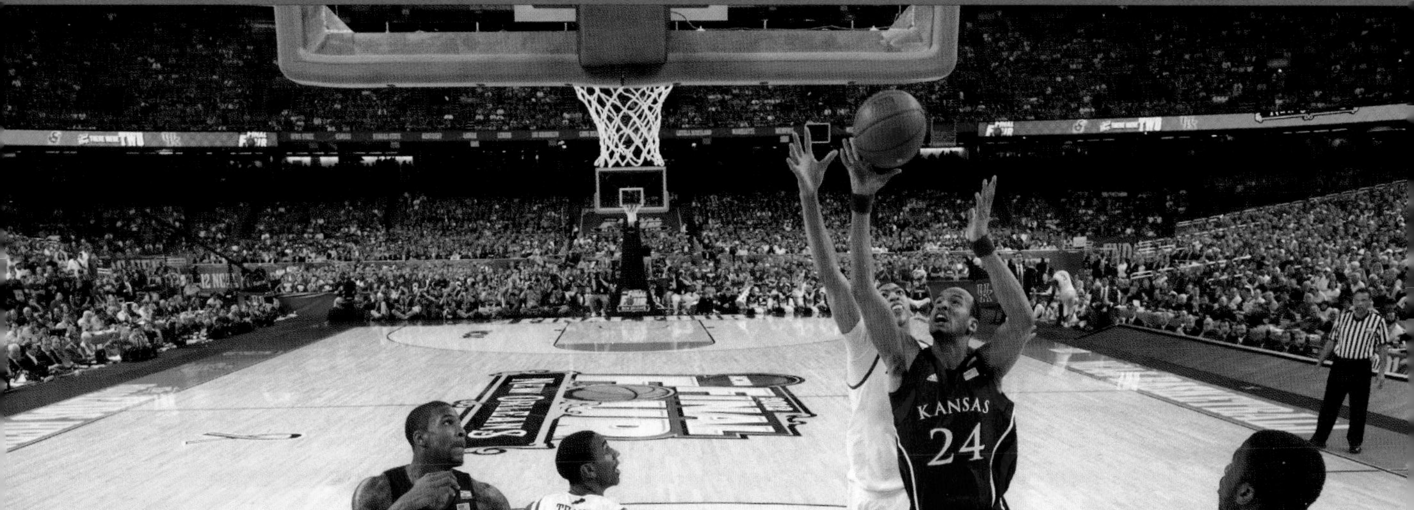

www.av2books.com

Go to www.av2books.com, and enter this book's unique code.

BOOK CODE

X546517

AV² by Weigl brings you media enhanced books that support active learning.

AV² provides enriched content that supplements and complements this book. Weigl's AV² books strive to create inspired learning and engage young minds in a total learning experience.

Your AV² Media Enhanced books come alive with...

Audio
Listen to sections of the book read aloud.

Key Words
Study vocabulary, and complete a matching word activity.

Video
Watch informative video clips.

Quizzes
Test your knowledge.

Embedded Weblinks
Gain additional information for research.

Slide Show
View images and captions, and prepare a presentation.

Try This!
Complete activities and hands-on experiments.

... and much, much more!

Published by AV² by Weigl
350 5th Avenue, 59th Floor
New York, NY 10118

Website: www.av2books.com www.weigl.com

Library of Congress Cataloging-in-Publication Data
Bekkering, Annalise.
NCAA basketball / Annalise Bekkering.
p. cm. – (Pro sports championships)
Includes index.
ISBN 978-1-62127-366-0 (hardcover : alk. paper) – ISBN 978-1-62127-371-4 (softcover : alk. paper)
1. NCAA Basketball Tournament—History—Juvenile literature. I. Title.
GV885.49.N37B45 2013
796.323'63—dc23
2012043079

Printed in the United States of America in North Mankato, Minnesota
1 2 3 4 5 6 7 8 9 0 17 16 15 14 13

012013
WEP301112

PROJECT COORDINATOR Aaron Carr EDITOR Steve Macleod ART DIRECTOR Terry Paulhus

Weigl acknowledges Getty Images as its primary image supplier for this title.

CONTENTS

What is the NCAA Basketball Championship?

The National **Collegiate** Athletic Association (NCAA) basketball championship is held every year. University and college basketball teams compete to play in the tournament. Winning the event is **prestigious**. The final game is one of the most popular sporting events in the United States.

The NCAA oversees most college and university sports in the United States. More than 1,000 schools are members of the NCAA. Member schools are divided into three divisions. Division I is made up of the largest schools.

The University of Kansas Jayhawks have played in the NCAA basketball tournament 41 times. They became champions in 1952, 1988, and 2008.

Division II and Division III schools are smaller. All three divisions host championship games. The Division I championship is the most popular. All of the athletes that compete in the NCAA are students. They have academic responsibilities to maintain. Athletes must achieve high grades to be able to play sports for their school.

CHANGES THROUGHOUT THE YEARS	
PAST	**PRESENT**
In 1939, there was an audience of 5,500 people for the final game.	In 2011, attendance at the final game was 70,913.
In 1977, the average ticket price was $7.78.	In 2008, the average ticket price was $77.92.
In 1946, about 500,000 people watched the final game on television.	In 2010, more than 23.9 million people watched the championship game on television.

Trophies

The NCAA championship-winning team receives two trophies. One trophy is gold-plated. It is a National Championship trophy awarded by the NCAA. The other trophy is from the National Association of Basketball Coaches. It is made out of Waterford crystal. This trophy is shaped like a basketball.

NCAA Basketball History

Dr. James Naismith invented basketball in 1891, in Springfield, Massachusetts. He created the game for students to play inside during the winter. The game was played with a soccer ball. Peach baskets were hung at each end of the gymnasium. Players would climb up a ladder to get the ball from the baskets. The bottom of the baskets was cut out so the ball would fall to the ground.

The head of the physical education department gave Dr. James Naismith 14 days to invent an indoor sport.

Basketball became popular very quickly. The first college game with five players on each side was played in 1896. The University of Chicago beat the University of Iowa 15–12. About 90 colleges in the United States had basketball teams by 1900.

The Intercollegiate Athletic Association of the United States (IAAUS) formed in 1906. The organization was created to oversee college sports. It became the National Collegiate Athletic Association (NCAA) four years later. More the 360 colleges had basketball teams by 1914.

The first national basketball tournament was hosted in Kansas City, Missouri, in 1937. However, all of teams came from the midwest instead of from across the nation. The National Invitational Tournament (NIT) held its first event in 1938. The tournament was held in New York. It received attention across the country. The first NCAA tournament was held the following year. It was organized by the National Association of Basketball Coaches (NABC). They wanted to bring more attention to basketball in the western states. The NCAA took over the tournament the next year.

In 1946, Oklahoma State beat out North Carolina in the championship game. They only won by three points.

At first, both NIT and NCAA tournaments were popular. The NCAA championship later became the ultimate college basketball tournament.

NCAA basketball had eight districts for the first 12 years. One team from each district played in the basketball tournament. The NCAA tournament has grown to include 68 teams. The NCAA basketball championship is also called March Madness. It is one of the biggest sporting events in the United States.

Basketball Cheers

Basketball fans have different chants and cheers for their favorite teams. Many universities have a school song. These songs are part of a school tradition. The University of Ohio song is called, "Stand Up and Cheer."

Rules of the Game

Basketball rules have changed since the sport was invented in 1891. Some leagues have different rules, but the game is similar wherever it is played.

1 The Game

NCAA basketball games have two halves. Each half is 20 minutes. There is a 15-minute break between halves. This is called halftime. The team with the highest score at the end of the game wins. If the score is tied at the end of the game, the teams play five minutes of overtime. Each team is allowed five players on the court at once. These five players play **offense** and **defense**.

2 Beginning the Game

Every basketball game begins with a jump ball. A player from each team faces off at center court. The other players line up around the circle at center. A referee tosses the ball in the air. The two players in the middle jump and try to knock the ball to one of their teammates.

3 Moving the Ball

There are two ways to move the basketball around the court. They are dribbling and passing. Dribbling is done by bouncing the ball against the floor. Players must dribble the ball to move around the court. If a player takes a step while holding the ball it is called traveling. This is against the rules. Basketball players pass to their teammates by throwing the ball through the air. They can also bounce the ball to their teammates.

4 Scoring

A team scores points by shooting the ball into the basket. A team scores two points for a shot taken close to the hoop. A team scores three points for a shot from behind the three-point line. The offensive team has 35 seconds to shoot the ball at the net in NCAA basketball. The defensive team tries to stop the other team from scoring. They try to block shots and passes. They can also try to steal control of the ball.

5 Fouls

The referee calls a foul when there is illegal contact between players. A foul can be called for pushing, tripping, or holding. If an offensive player is fouled while shooting, they get to take a foul shot. The player stands at a special place on the court called the free throw line. A foul shot is worth one point. A player can also get a technical foul for unsportsmanlike behavior.

Making the Call

There are three referees for NCAA basketball games. They make sure players are following the rules. A referee must know all of the rules of basketball. The referee stops the game by blowing a whistle when a rule is broken. Referees run up and down the court to watch the players. A referee must be able to make decisions very quickly.

The Basketball Court

Basketball is played on a rectangular court. It is 94 feet (28.7 meters) long by 50 feet (15.2 m) wide. There is a basket at each end of the court. The basket is 18 inches (45.7 centimeters) in diameter. The backboard behind the basket is 3.5 or 4 feet (1.1 or 1.2 m) high by 6 feet (1.8 m) wide.

There is a rectangular box drawn on the floor at each end of the court. This box is 19 feet (5.8 m) long by 12 feet (3.7 m) wide. This area is called the key. Offensive players are only allowed to stand in the key for three seconds. The free throw line is at the top of the key. It is 15 feet (4.6 m) from the backboard.

The three-point line in NCAA basketball is an **arced** line 20 feet and 9 inches (6.3 m) from the basket. Any shot made from behind this line is worth three points.

Basketball can be played on many different surfaces. Outdoor games can be played on asphalt or concrete. In gymnasiums and arenas, basketball courts often have hardwood floors. Some indoor courts are made out of flexible, interlocking tiles.

The center circle is often replaced with a logo. This can be a team's logo or the logo of the tournament, such as the NCAA Final Four.

Players on the Team

Each basketball team has five players on the court at one time. Each member of the team has different strengths and skills. All teammates play both offense and defense. On offense, the point guard is usually small and fast, and has excellent ball handling and passing skills. The shooting guard is often very quick, and is good at scoring and passing. The small forward is good at scoring both near and far from the net. The power forward is normally big and strong. This player needs good defensive and **rebounding** skills. The center is usually the tallest player on the team. Centers score many points near the net and block shots on defense. The coach is an important part of the team. This person is in charge of strategy and instructing players.

THE BASKETBALL COURT

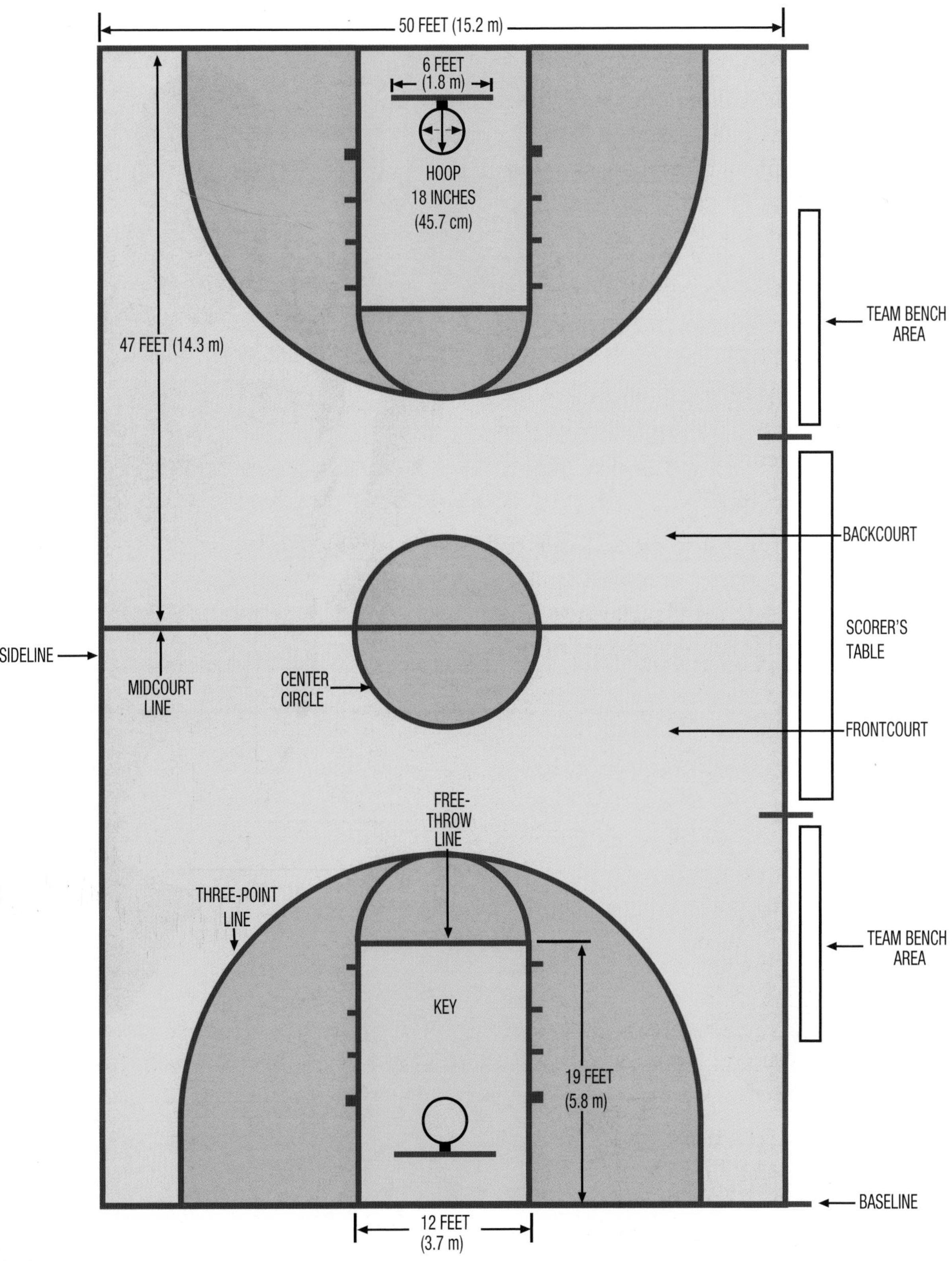

Basketball Equipment

Playing basketball requires very little equipment. This is one of the reasons it is such a popular sport. People of different ages and skill levels can play basketball.

The most important piece of equipment is a basketball. The ball is usually made of nylon or leather, and is orange or brown in color. The surface of the ball is pebbled. This rough surface allows players to grip the ball. A men's basketball is 29.5 to 30 inches (74.9 to 76.2 cm) in **circumference** and weighs 20 to 22 ounces (567 to 624 grams).

Most players wear high-top shoes. Basketball players move around a lot and make quick movements from side-to-side. Having high-top shoes helps prevent players from injuring their ankles.

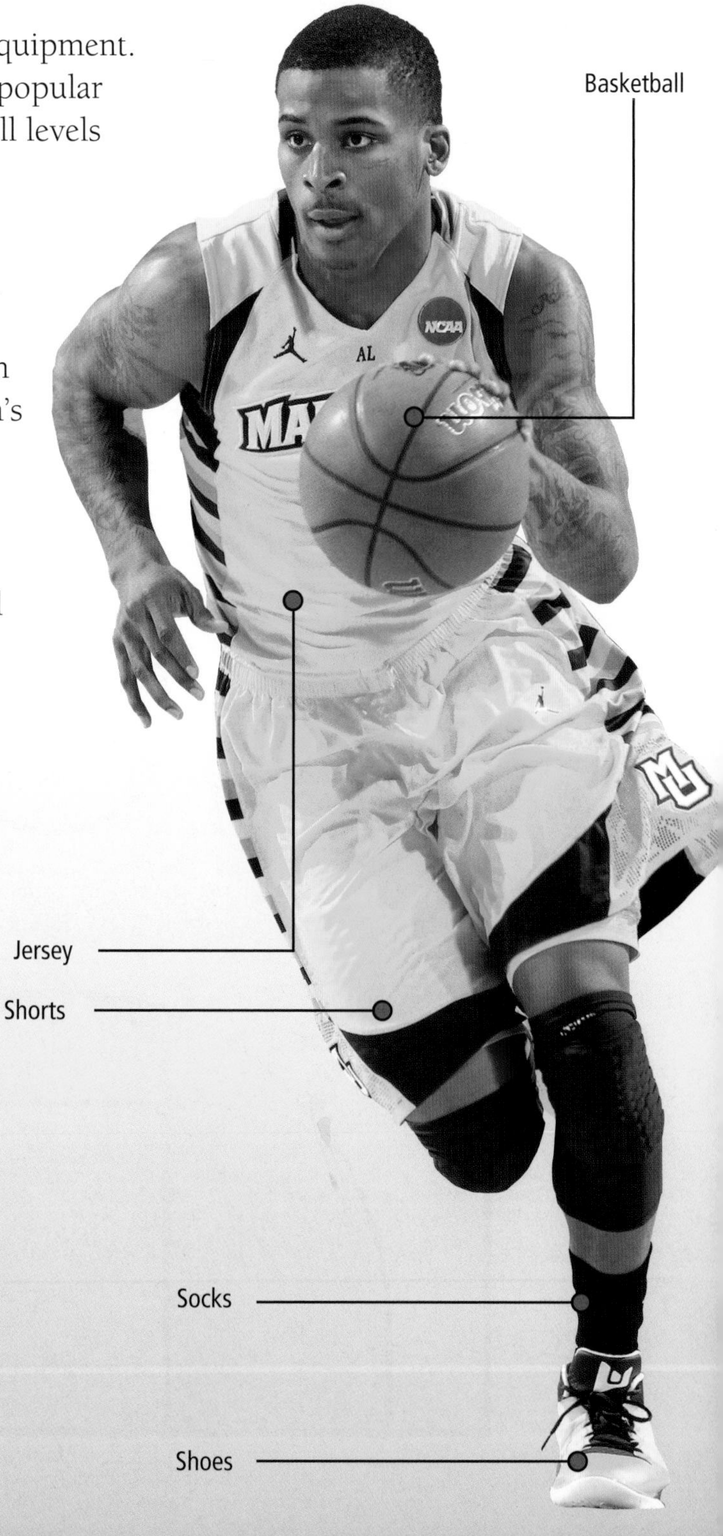

Basketball

Jersey

Shorts

Socks

Shoes

The basketball used in women's games is slightly smaller. It is 28.5 to 29 inches (72.4 to 73.7 cm) in circumference and weighs 18 to 20 ounces (510 to 567 grams).

The basket is another important piece of equipment. The rim is made out of metal and has a diameter of 18 inches (45.7 cm). The net below is made from nylon. In outdoor basketball, the net is sometimes made out of chains. The basket is attached to a backboard made of plastic or glass. Sometimes players try to bounce the ball off the backboard to get the ball to fall into the basket.

Team Uniforms

Most basketball uniforms have a sleeveless top and shorts in the team's colors. The uniforms are made out of synthetic, or humanmade, materials, such as nylon, polyester, or rayon. Players have a number on the front and back of their uniform. In the NCAA, the players can have the numbers 00, 0 to 15, 20 to 25, 30 to 35, 40 to 45, or 50 to 55. Sometimes, the player's last name is written on the back of the uniform above the number. In the NCAA, each team has a light-colored uniform and a dark-colored uniform. The home team wears the light uniform. The visiting team wears the dark uniform.

Qualifying to Play

The Division I final tournament is called the Final Four. The road to the Final Four takes place over three weeks in March and April every year. Sixty-eight teams qualify for the NCAA championship tournament. The selection of these teams is a complicated process. There are 31 **conferences** in the NCAA that automatically have one team qualify for the championship tournament. Every conference has its own tournament. Each winning team qualifies as one of the 68 teams to play in the NCAA championship tournament. A committee selects the remaining 37 teams. They try to choose the country's best teams for the tournament.

The NCAA Men's Basketball Championship started out with eight teams competing in 1939. Today, 68 teams play in the championship.

The committee chooses eight of the lowest ranked teams to play against each other. This round of games is called the First Four. The four winning teams of the First Four move on to the first round of the NCAA tournament. The committee arranges the teams in a **bracket**. The bracket determines which teams will play each other based on region and rank.

UCLA has played in the Final Four 18 times. They have won the NCAA tournament 11 times. This is more than any other school.

The University of Pittsburgh Panthers have played in the NCAA tournament 23 times. They made it to the Final Four once, but did not win.

In the first round, there are four regional tournaments of 16 teams each. The four regions are East, West, South, and Midwest.

In each region, the highest-ranked teams play against the lowest-ranked teams. Once a team loses a game it is out of the competition. The winning teams move on to the next round.

There are 32 teams in the second round of the tournament. Each team plays another team, and the winners move on to the next round. Winners continue playing each other until there are only four teams left in the tournament. These four teams are the regional champions. They play in the national semi-finals, known as the Final Four. The winners of this round play each other for the championship.

The Net

Cutting down the net is an NCAA tradition for the championship team. Each player from the winning team cuts a piece of the basketball net. The coach cuts the last piece. Each player keeps a small piece of the net as a souvenir, and the coach keeps the rest.

Where They Play

The NCAA basketball championship game is a major event. Many cities compete for the opportunity to host the Final Four. The first NCAA tournament was held at Patten Gymnasium in Evanston, Illinois. The national championship game has been played in Kansas City, Missouri, more times than any other city. It has been played there 10 times. The biggest crowd for an NCAA championship final was in 2009 in Detroit. There were 72,922 people there to watch North Carolina defeat Michigan State 89–72.

The host city is chosen a few years in advance. This gives the city time to prepare for the big event. The Final Four event draws large crowds. Since 1996 every championship series has been played in a football dome stadium, instead of a basketball arena to accommodate more people.

Mascots and cheerleaders perform in support of their team.

The University of Kentucky Wildcats won their eighth NCAA tournament championship in 2012. They defeated Kansas 67–59 at the Superdome in New Orleans.

The University of Baylor women's basketball team won 40 games and had zero losses on their way to winning the 2012 women's Final Four in Denver. They are the first NCAA women's or men's team to go 40-0.

NCAA Championship Winners 2003–2012

YEAR	LOCATION	WINNING TEAM	SCORE	RUNNER-UP
2012	New Orleans	Kentucky	67–59	Kansas
2011	Houston	Connecticut	54–41	Butler
2010	Indianapolis	Duke	61–59	Butler
2009	Detroit	North Carolina	89–72	Michigan State
2008	San Antonio	Kansas	75–68	Memphis
2007	Atlanta	Florida	84–75	Ohio State
2006	Indianapolis	Florida	73–57	UCLA
2005	St. Louis	North Carolina	75–70	Illinois
2004	San Antonio	Connecticut	82–73	Georgia Tech
2003	New Orleans	Syracuse	81–78	Kansas

Mapping NCAA Champions

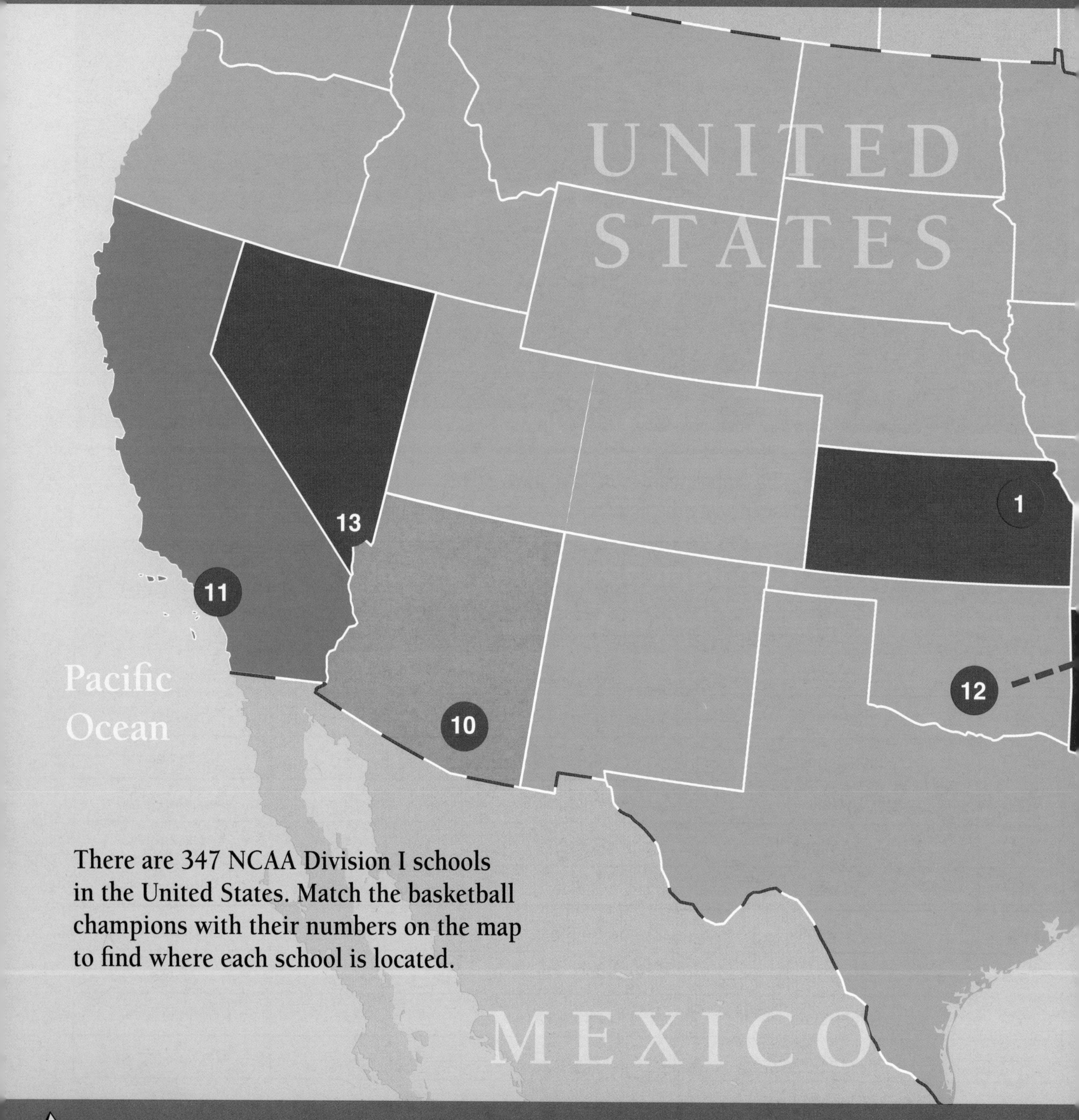

There are 347 NCAA Division I schools in the United States. Match the basketball champions with their numbers on the map to find where each school is located.

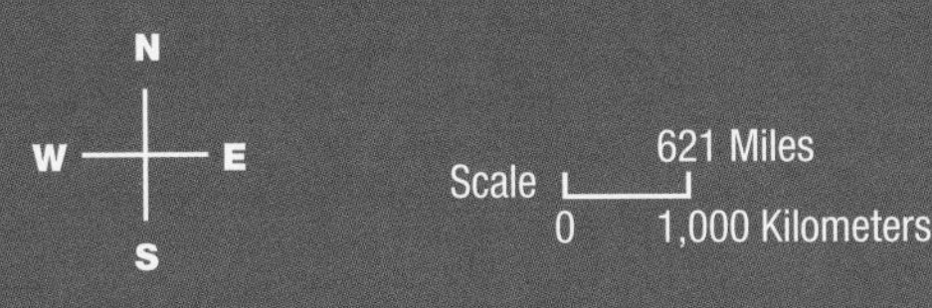

CANADA

Atlantic Ocean

20 8 14 5 4 17 6 18 15 9 16 7 3 19 2

NCAA Division I Champions Since 1967

1 University of Kansas
2 University of Florida
3 University of North Carolina
4 University of Connecticut
5 Syracuse University
6 University of Maryland
7 Duke University
8 Michigan State University
9 University of Kentucky
10 University of Arizona
11 UCLA
12 University of Arkansas
13 UNLV
14 University of Michigan
15 Indiana University
16 University of Louisville
17 Villanova University
18 Georgetown University
19 North Carolina State University
20 Marquette University

Women and Basketball

At first, women's basketball was not a popular sport. In 1892, women's basketball had its own set of rules. Women played the first basketball tournament using men's rules in 1926. The first five-player, full-court women's game was played in 1971.

In 1972, the government passed a law called Title IX. This rule said schools had to fund men's and women's sports equally. Women's sports programs began to grow. In 1978, the Association for Intercollegiate Athletics for Women (AIAW) televised their championship. The Women's Basketball League (WBL), a women's professional league, was also formed that year.

The number of girls competing in high school sports also increased. By 1972, about 2.7 percent of girls participated in school sports. Today, 40 percent of girls participate in school sports.

The AIAW ended in 1982 and the NCAA took control over women's college sports. That year, Louisiana Tech defeated Cheney State 76–62, to win the first NCAA Division I Women's Basketball championship.

Millions of fans watch the women's NCAA championship every year. The championship follows the same format as the men's tournament.

The University of Tennessee has won the women's NCAA tournament eight times since 1982.

Women's basketball became very popular in the 1990s. The Women's National Basketball Association (WNBA) was formed in 1997. This league gives top female college players the opportunity to play professional basketball in the United States.

Today, women's basketball is played with the same rules as men's basketball. There are a few differences. A smaller ball used in women's games. Also, the three-point line is one foot closer to the basket in women's NCAA games than in men's NCAA games.

The New York Liberty played against the Los Angeles Sparks during the inaugural WNBA game in 1997. New York won 67–57.

Diana Taurasi

Diana Taurasi had one of the most successful college careers in women's basketball. She played for the University of Connecticut for four years from 2000 to 2004. Her team won the NCAA championship three of those years. In college, Taurasi averaged 15 points, 4.5 assists, and 4.3 rebounds per game. She was named the Naismith National Player of the Year in 2003 and 2004. Taurasi was the first draft pick in the 2004 WNBA draft. She currently plays for the Phoenix Mercury. She was named the USA Basketball Female Athlete of the Year in 2006 and 2010.

Historical Highlights

Some of the greatest basketball players in the world have played in the NCAA basketball championship. These players have created memorable moments in the tournament. Some championship games have been won and lost in the final seconds.

Beginning in 1962, coach John Wooden led UCLA to 13 Final Four tournaments in 15 years. His team won the championship 10 times. UCLA won the NCAA championship seven years in a row from 1967 to 1973.

After Michigan state beat Indiana State, Magic Johnson was voted Most Outstanding Player of the Final Four for his extraordinary effort in the game.

In 1979, Earvin "Magic" Johnson and Michigan State defeated Larry Bird and Indiana State in the NCAA championship. Magic Johnson and Larry Bird both went on to become superstars in the National Basketball Association (NBA).

In 1983, the North Carolina State Wolfpack played the University of Houston in the championship game. Houston was favored to win, and North Carolina State was the **underdog**. In the final few seconds of the game, Lorenzo Charles of North Carolina State made a surprise basket. He scored a **slam dunk**, and the Wolfpack won the game 54–52.

Syracuse led Indiana 73–72 with 28 seconds left in the 1987 championship game. Syracuse was closely guarding Indiana's best shooter, Steve Alford, so he could not get the ball and score. An Indiana player saw that Keith Smart was open near the baseline and passed him the ball. With four seconds left on the clock, Smart made the shot, and Indiana won the championship 74–73.

In the 2003 championship game, Kansas was down by three points to Syracuse. With only two seconds left in the game, Michael Lee of Kansas took a shot from the three-point line. Hakim Warrick of Syracuse blocked the ball and knocked it out of bounds. Syracuse won the game 81–78.

Keith Smart cut down part of the net after helping his team win the 1987 national title.

NCAA CHAMPIONSHIP RECORDS

RECORD	PLAYER	TEAM	YEAR(S)
Points (44)	Bill Walton	UCLA	1973
Points by a Freshman (26)	Toby Bailey	UCLA	1995
Field Goals (21)	Bill Walton	UCLA	1973
Free Throws Made (18)	Gail Goodrich	UCLA	1965
Three-Pointers Made (7)	Steve Alford, Dave Sieger, Tony Delk	Indiana, Oklahoma, Kentucky	1987, 1988, 1996
Assists (11)	Rumeal Robinson	Michigan	1989
Rebounds (27)	Bill Russell	San Francisco	1956
Blocked Shots (6)	Joakim Noah	Florida	2006
Steals (8)	Ty Lawson	North Carolina	2009

LEGENDS and Current Stars

Wilt Chamberlain – Center

Wilt Chamberlain attended the University of Kansas and played for the Jayhawks from 1956 to 1959. He averaged 29.9 points and 18.3 rebounds per game during his college career. At 7 foot 1 inch (215 cm), the NCAA added rules so that Chamberlain did not have an advantage over other players. Chamberlain never won an NCAA championship. In his sophomore year, his team lost the championship in triple overtime. Although his team lost, Chamberlain was named the most valuable player (MVP) of the tournament. Chamberlain played professional basketball in the NBA from 1959 to 1973. He won two NBA championships and set many records. In one game, he scored 100 points. This remains the highest individual score in NBA history.

Wilt Chamberlain

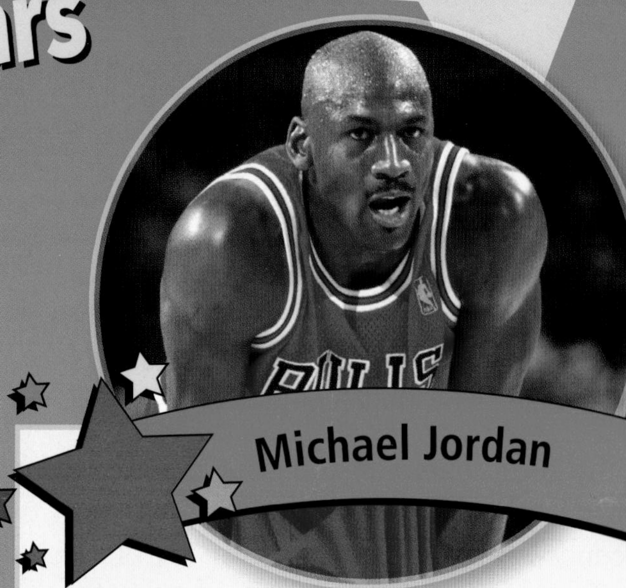

Michael Jordan

Michael Jordan – Guard

Michael Jordan is one of basketball's most recognizable players. He played for the University of North Carolina Tar Heels from 1981 to 1984. Jordan is known for one of the most memorable moments in NCAA championship history. In the 1982 NCAA championship game, he made a **jump shot** in the last second of the game to defeat Georgetown University 63–62. After college, Jordan spent many years playing for the Chicago Bulls in the NBA. He led the Bulls to six NBA championships and won six MVP awards.

Mario Chalmers – Guard

Mario Chalmers played for the University of Kansas Jayhawks from 2005 to 2008. He helped lead his team to the NCAA championship title in 2008. He was named the Most Outstanding Player of the Final Four that year. Chalmers is an extraordinary defensive player. In his final year with the team, he had 97 steals and 169 assists. Chalmers is known for one of the most memorable plays in the NCAA championships. In the 2008 championship game against Memphis, he made a three-point shot with 2.1 seconds left, tying the game. His team then won in overtime. Chalmers joined the NBA in 2008 and currently plays for the Miami Heat. He helped the Heat win the NBA championship in 2012.

Carmelo Anthony – Forward

Carmelo Anthony played one year of college basketball. In the 2002–2003 season, he led Syracuse University to its first ever NCAA championship victory. He set the school record for points by a freshman in a season with 607 points and set the Big East Conference record for points per game by a rookie at 22.5. In the championship game versus Kansas, Anthony had 20 points, 10 rebounds, and seven assists. Syracuse won the game 81–78. Anthony was named the tournament's most valuable player. He was the third freshman to win the award. Anthony has played for the Denver Nuggets and the New York Knicks during his nine-year NBA career. He has been one of the top 10 point scorers in seven of those seasons and has been named an all-star five times.

Famous Firsts

The term "March Madness" was first used in 1939 by H.V. Porter to describe the Illinois high school basketball finals. The term began to be used for the NCAA championship tournament in the 1980s.

In 1946, the championship game was televised for the first time. Oklahoma State defeated North Carolina, and the game was shown on New York local television. About 500,000 people watched the game. The championship game was televised nationally for the first time 1954.

In 1952, Seattle was the first city to host the Final Four, with the semi-finals and finals taking place in the same city.

The University of Maryland became the first school to beat five former NCAA champions on their path to win the championship in 2002.

In 2004, the men's and women's teams from the University of Connecticut both won the NCAA championship. This was the first time that both the men's and women's teams from the same school won the title in the same year.

In 1984, John Thompson, Jr. became the first African American coach to win the NCAA championship, when Georgetown University defeated Houston.

In 1997, the University of Arizona became the first team to defeat three number one teams to win the championship.

The first time the top four **seeded** teams made it to the Final Four was in 2008. The teams were Kansas, Memphis, UCLA, and North Carolina. Kansas won the championship.

The First NCAA Championship Game

The first NCAA championship game was held at the Patten Gymnasium in Evanston, Illinois, on March 27, 1939. Oregon defeated Ohio State 46–43. Oregon dominated the rebounds and moved quicker down the court than Ohio State. John Dick from Oregon was the team's high scorer with 13 points. About 5,500 people attended the game.

The Rise of the Championship

1891

Dr. James Naismith invents basketball.

1939

The first NCAA championship takes place. The University of Oregon wins the championship.

1946

Oklahoma State becomes the first team to win two championships in a row.

1953

The tournament expands from 16 to 22 teams.

1954

The NCAA championship game is televised nationally for the first time.

1966

Texas Western University wins the championship. They are the first team with an all African American starting lineup.

1973

UCLA's coach John Wooden leads his team to the first of seven NCAA championship titles in a row. Thirty-nine million people watch the championship game on television.

1975

The tournament expands to 32 teams.

1980

The tournament expands to 48 teams.

1985

The tournament expands to 64 teams. Villanova, the eighth-seeded team, becomes the lowest-seeded team to ever win the NCAA championship.

1986

LSU advances to the Final Four as a number 11 seed team. They become the lowest-seeded team to ever play in the final round of the tournament.

2001

The tournament expands to 65 teams. Almost 16 million people watch the televised championship game.

2011

The NCAA tournament expands to 68 teams. No number one seeded teams make it to the Final Four. It is only the second time this has happened since the tournament expanded to 53 teams in 1984.

QUICK FACTS

- Dr. Naismith also developed the basketball program at the University of Kansas.
- In 1950, City College of New York entered both the NIT and NCAA championships, and won both tournaments.
- The NCAA championship is also known as "The Big Dance."

Test Your Knowledge

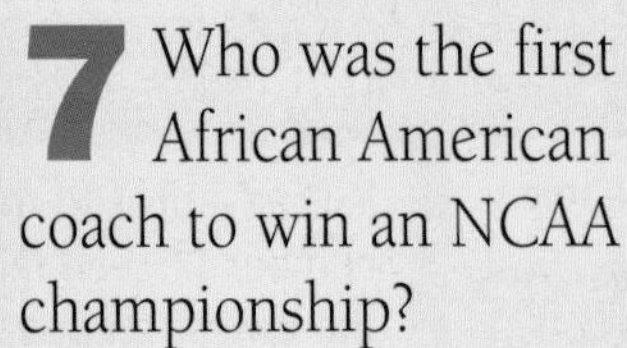

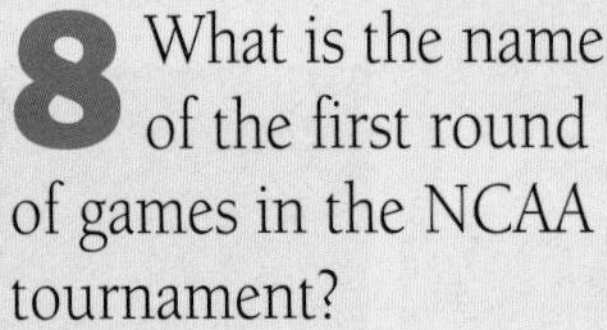

1 Who invented basketball, and in what year?

2 Which was the first team to win the NCAA championship in 1939?

3 How many people attended the final NCAA game in 2011?

4 How many NCAA Division I schools are there in the United States?

5 What university team did Michael Jordan play for?

6 How many referees are there in an NCAA basketball game?

7 Who was the first African American coach to win an NCAA championship?

8 What is the name of the first round of games in the NCAA tournament?

9 Name one person who holds the record for most three-point shots made during an NCAA championship game.

10 Which is the lowest-seeded team to ever win the NCAA championship?

Answers: 1.) Dr. James Naismith in 1891 2.) University of Oregon 3.) There were 70,913 people in attendance 4.) 347 5.) University of North Carolina Tar Heels 6.) Three 7.) John Thompson, Jr. 8.) The First Four 9.) Steve Alford, Dave Sieger, and Tony Delk all made seven three-point shots in NCAA championship games 10.) Villanova in 1985

Key Words

arced: curved, like an arch

bracket: a diagram showing a series of games in a tournament

circumference: the distance around an object

collegiate: having to do with college or college students

conferences: groups of sports teams

defense: the team that is trying to keep another team from scoring

jump shot: a shot that is made while the player is jumping

offense: the team that has the ball and is trying to score points

prestigious: having high status and a good reputation

rebounding: grabbing the ball after it bounces off the rim or the backboard

seeded: how a team is ranked in a tournament

slam dunk: a shot made when the player stuffs the ball through the basket

three-point line: a half circle around the center of the basket

underdog: the team with a disadvantage that is expected to lose

Index

Log on to www.av2books.com

AV² by Weigl brings you media enhanced books that support active learning. Go to www.av2books.com, and enter the special code found on page 2 of this book. You will gain access to enriched and enhanced content that supplements and complements this book. Content includes video, audio, weblinks, quizzes, a slide show, and activities.

AV² Online Navigation

Book Pages
AV² pages directly correspond to pages in the book.

Audio
Listen to sections of the book read aloud.

Video
Watch informative video clips.

Embedded Weblinks
Gain additional information for research.

Key Words
Study vocabulary, and complete a matching word activity.

Try This!
Complete activities and hands-on experiments.

Quizzes
Test your knowledge.

Slide Show
View images and captions, and prepare a presentation.

AV² was built to bridge the gap between print and digital. We encourage you to tell us what you like and what you want to see in the future.

Sign up to be an AV² Ambassador at www.av2books.com/ambassador.

Due to the dynamic nature of the Internet, some of the URLs and activities provided as part of AV² by Weigl may have changed or ceased to exist. AV² by Weigl accepts no responsibility for any such changes. All media enhanced books are regularly monitored to update addresses and sites in a timely manner. Contact AV² by Weigl at 1-866-649-3445 or av2books@weigl.com with any questions, comments, or feedback.